Just A Passing Moment In Time:

A Journey of Life and Death in Haiku

Brett C. Persson

Just A Passing Moment In Time

A Journey of Life and Dead in Haiku

brettcpersson@gmail.com

www.brettcpersson.com

X: @brettcpersson

Nudous Publishing, LLC

www.nudouspublishing.com
info@nudouspublishing.com

Paperback ISBN: 978-1-964793-75-7

To My Wife:

From the moment I met you, I knew that you were special. You had a twinkle in your eye that just made me smile. Over the years, we've shared so many wonderful memories together. Through everything, you've always been my rock. You've been by my side through good times and bad, and I can't imagine my life without you. That's why this book is dedicated to you, my beautiful wife. Thank you for everything. I love you from the bottom of my heart.

To My Kids:

This book is dedicated to my three daughters: Kinsey, Sara, and Baylie. You are the lights of my life. You have brought me more happiness than I ever could have imagined. You are my reason for everything. I love you all so much. Thank you for being who you are and for everything that you do. I am so proud of each and every one of you. Thank you for always being there for me, no matter what. I love you all from the bottom of my heart.

To My Parents:

No one knows the pain and suffering of addiction like those who have to watch a loved one go through it. For my parents, that person was me. Through the years, they've seen me at my worst. Yet, despite all that I put them through, they never gave up on me. They were always there to support me, whether in the middle of a relapse or fighting my way back to sobriety. I know I can never repay them for all they've done, but I can try to make their sacrifice worth it by living my life in a way that honors their love and support. I want to say thank you to my parents for being my rock during the hardest times of my life. Thank you for never giving up on me. Thank you for being the light in my darkness.

Table of Contents

Year 0

He Swims To Meet Her
Searching Throughout The Darkness
They Bond Together

Potential Life Starts
Started By A Single Spark
Growing, Dividing

Splitting, Traveling
Implanting Within The Wall
Now An Embryo

Weeks Begin To Pass
Early Developed Fetus
Developing Life

Features Beginning

Life Forming Within The Womb

Heart Lightly Beating

Gender Develops

Arms, Hands, Fingers, Feet, And Toes

Now Four Inches Long

Yawning And Stretching

Audible Fetal Heartbeat

Now Six Inches Long

Hair begins To Grow

Ten Inches, Up To A Pound

Creation Halfway

Hearing Developed
Responding To Stimuli
Fourteen Inches Long

Lungs Still Immature
Brain Develops Rapidly
Eighteen Inches Long

Grasps, Blinks, Turns His Head
Coordinated Reflex
Preparing For Birth

The Moment Arrives
Born Of Woman Into World
Soul Born From To Light

Year 1

He Arrives Crying
Now Exposed To This New World
Life Has Now Begun

Nurses From Mother
Adjusting, Bonding, Living
Sleep, Poop, Cry, Repeat

Looking And Seeing
Grasping At Papa's Finger
People Gather Near

Adoring Him So
Celebration Of New Life
Family And Friends

Swaddled Up So Tight
Reminding Him Of His Home
Comfort And Soothing

The First Diaper Rash
His Head And Neck Grow Stronger
He Smiles, And Coos

Reacts To Faces
Growing And Developing
He Responds And Laughs

He Stands With Some Help
He Greets Loved Ones With A Smile
Baby Boy Growing

Pain In His Mouth Starts
His Teeth Tearing Through His Gums
Unsure Of The Pain

Drooling And Fussy
Miserable For First Time
Is This What Life Is

Starting To Babble
Pain Of Needles Puncturing
Solid Food Warms Him

Now Begins To Crawl
He Grows More And Has Tantrums
Trying To Learn More

Mommy, Juice, Eat, Up
Small Commands Now Understood
Brain Developing

Year 2

Playing Patty Cake
Calls His Mama And Dada
Place A Block In Cup

He Pulls To A Stand
Cruising Around The Table
Bang, His Head Hit Hard

Mama Cries And Holds
First Injury Scares Them Both
He Is Being Held

First Pain And Then Love
Is This What Life Will Be Like
Always Pain, Then Love

Taking Toys From Friend
Interacting With Others
Clapping, And Hugging

First Few Steps Taken
He Begins To Feed Himself
Able To Stack Blocks

Walks Away From Mom
Looking Back To See Her There
He Points To Show Things

Assisting When Dressed
He Sits And Looks At A Book
Baby To Toddler

He Sees His Mama
She Sweeps, And So He Does Too
Starts To Use A Spoon

He Climbs Up On Chair
He Falls Climbing Down From It
Mild Pain And Still Cries

He Runs, Kicks A Ball
Putting Words Together Now
Toy Food On Toy Plate

Year 3

The Terrible Twos
He Is Not Sure What That Means
But Hears Them Say It

Reacts To Others
Upset When Someone Is Hurt
Gestures, Waves, And Points

Starting To Walk Stairs
Following Routines So Soon
Is This What Life Is

He Removes His Shirt
Jumping, Pointing, Loosens Pants
Just Because He Can

Joins Others To Play
He Knows His Name And Responds
Starts Using A Fork

He Knows His Colors
Can Strings Items Together
Motor Skills Improve

Can Make A Circle
Sees Mom And Dad Fight Sometimes
Seems Scary To Him

Year 4

Can Follow Commands
He Stretches Out And Screamed At
Don't Touch The Hot Stove

Mama Always Here
Dada Is Never Around
At Something Called Work

He Sits In Her Lap
She Reads, He Points At Pictures
They Laugh Together

He Works On Puzzles
He Dances In The Sprinkler
Joyful And Fun Times

Bath Time Is Play Time
Splashing Around And Laughing
Mama Laughs With Him

Notices She Leaves
Mama Left Home Without Him
He Is Sad And Scared

Joy When She Returns
From Sadness To Happiness
Missing Her When Gone

Build A Fort With Dad
He Bounces On Daddy's Back
Fun When Dad Is Home

Year 5

He Pretends All Day
He Is A Superhero
Fighting The Bad Guys

Enjoys Games He Plays
He Asks For His Friend Billy
Wants Interaction

His Sentences Grow
Forming More Complexity
Plays Catch With His Dad

He Knows His Colors
Usually Pours His Milk
Unbuttons His Coat

A Child's Sweetest Laugh
He Draws Using His Left Hand
His Mind Evolving

He Draws Stick Figures
He Loves His Dog Ariel
They Nap Together

He Falls Off The Swing
Blinding Pain In His Right Arm
He Screams And Bellows

Mama Crying Too
Sirens Louder Than His Screams
They Take Us Away

Dad Comes Home Early
He Is Crying; Dad Hugs Him
The Boy Is Happy

His First Broken Bone
His Parents Both Sign The Cast
The Pain Is Better

Year 6

He Takes Turns Playing
Singing And Dancing, Poorly
Feeling Wild And Free

They Send Him Away
He Is In Kindergarten
Scared Of Being There

Adjustment Issues
Hard Being Away From Home
Anxiety Builds

Mama Reassures
Is Going To Be Okay
He Is Still Afraid

With Time He Adjusts

Realizes He Likes It

Learning And Growing

Excelling At School

Teacher Says He Can Count Well

Learning His Letters

Can Hop On One Foot

Always Excited For School

He Knows Day From Night

Year 7

Tying His Own Shoes
Dad Starts To Teach Him Guitar
Moves With The Music

Now In The First Grade
He Excels At His Studies
Love To Run, Skip, Hop

Learns To Ride A Bike
Personality Showing
Bonding With His Dad

Making Friends At School
Mind Expanding Rapidly
Starting To Reason

Confident And Sure
Liked By Teachers And Students
Enjoys Coloring

Loves Telling Bad Jokes
Wondering What Will Be Next
Loving And Caring

Year 8

Getting Much Stronger
Is Always Active Outside
Energy Abounds

Helps Mom In Kitchen
Starting To Run With His Dad
Still Playing Guitar

Asking Good Questions
Enjoys School And Learning Things
Socially Aware

Understands Money
Saving His Allowance Up
Is Sometimes Grouchy

Wants To Please Others
Sometimes He Grows Impatient
Shows Love For Others

Joined Little League Team
Enjoys Playing With Teammates
He Plays First Base Well

Eating Healthy Foods
Dad Teaching Him Nutrition
Mom Teaching Cooking

Year 9

Happy, Fun, And Free
Sometimes He Will Get Upset
Working Hard To Learn

Scared At Night Sometimes
When Mom And Dad Start To Fight
Mostly They Just Love

Takes After His Dad
Leader Not A Follower
Kids Look Up To Him

Mom Cries, Her Dad Died
Doesn't Really Understand
Sad By Grandpa's Death

They Dress In All Black
 Standing Out In The Hot Sun
Everyone Is Sad

Life's First Death For Him
As Time Passes, He Forgets
Life Will Remind Him

Year 10

Life Gets In A Rhythm
Moving Forward, Progressing
Absorbing Knowledge

Improves In Baseball
Gets Better Playing Guitar
Jams With The Old Man

Runs Almost Daily
Getting Stronger And Leaner
Parents Very Proud

Has Trouble At School
Sticking Up For His Best Friend
Fighting A Bully

Dad Is Mad And Proud
Feels Bad For Hurting Someone
Conflicted Feelings

Defending Others
Dad Talks About Right From Wrong
We Help When We Can

Year 11

Now In The Fifth Grade
Taller Than Most Of His Class
Understands The News

Getting Opinions
Talks Issues With His Parents
Thinking, Pondering

Pushes Boundaries
Making Mom And Dad Angry
Sometimes In Trouble

Feels He Is Special
Knows He Can Be Anything
Parents Supportive

Sad And Heart Broken
His Dog Ariel Passes
Life, Cruel And Mean

Time Goes On, Pain Fades
Continues To Learn And Grow
Appreciates Life

Year 12

Dad Takes Him Shooting
Powerful, Loud, And Awesome
Both Amazed And Scared

Must Learn How To Cook
Mom Teaches Him To Cook More
To Impress The Girls

Still Playing Baseball
Team Makes The Championship
Wins A Big Trophy

Feet Hitting Pavement
Joins A Fun Run With His Dad
They Do Well In Race

Teacher Pushes Him
Wanting Him To Push Limits
Takes On The Challenge

He Learns Easily
He Is Smart, And He Knows It
Proud, Not Arrogant

Watches A Space Launch
The Shuttle Soars Through The Air
Loud And Breath Taking

Year 13

Now In Middle School
Learn From Multiple Teachers
Learning So Much More

Hair Starting To Grow
His Body Is Changing Fast
Voice Starting To Change

Dad Gives Him 'The Talk'
Feeling Different With Girls
Attention From Them

Still Enjoying Sports
He Joins The School Wrestling Team
He Is Strong And Fast

Can Grasp Tone Of Voice

Understands Body Language

Sees Nonverbal Cues

He Dreams About Space

Looks To The Stars In Wonder

Explores Rocketry

Year 14

Flirting With The Girls
Body Continues To Change
He Explores Himself

A Talent For Math
The Numbers Come Easily
Engineering Spark

Thinks Outside The Box
Contemplates Many What If's
Mind Expanding Thoughts

The Shuttle Is Lost
First Teacher In Space Is Gone
Wonders What Happened

Confident And Sure
Wrestles For District Title
Does Well, But Loses

Feeling Of Failure
Down On Himself For Losing
Dad Reassures Him

Takes Girl To Movie
While Ferris Runs Around Town
He Kisses The Girl

First Kiss Is Special
Even After The Two Part
Will Never Forget

Year 15

Becoming Young Man
The Last Year Of Middle School
Challenges Ahead

Wanting More Knowledge
Becomes An Avid Reader
Getting More Knowledge

Focused On Studies
He Stops Wrestling For The Team
Continues To Run

Like To Socialize
Takes Out A Couple Of Girls
Nothing Serious

Interest Holds Strong

Watches Challenger Hearings

Faulty O-Rings Failed

Space Exploration

Building Armature Rockets

Launching Them With Dad

Strives To Do His Best

He Makes His Mom Proud Of Him

Successful Student

Testing For High School

Places High For Advanced Math

Is Labeled Gifted

Year 16

Gets Learners Permit
Dad Teaches Him How To Drive
Mom Worries For Him

High School Is Perfect
Great Studies And Greater Girls
The Private School Edge

Applies His Knowledge
Academic Excellence
The Top Of His Class

Learns Programming Skills
Excels With The Computer
Studies Computers

Discovery Launch
America Back To Space
Enthralled With Rockets

Hormones Are Raging
Spends Time With Different Girls
Advancing His Moves

Mind Focused And Sharp
Using His Love For Knowledge
Goals And Plans Set Forth

Year 17

Passed His Driving Test
Mom And Dad Get Him A Car
Used But It Is His

Provided For Him
A Reward For Doing Good
Driving Is Freeing

Pulse Is Racing Fast
Rounding Second Base To Third
Now Finding Third Base

Heat Builds In His Groin
Blood Surges Through His Body
Looks At Her, She Nods

They Lay Together
Both Out Of Breath And Happy
Sweaty And Giggling

He Feels Like A Man
High On The Experience
In Touch With His Heart

Relationship Builds
Is Getting More Serious
Parents Meet The Girl

Drunk At A Party
Euphoric Rush To The Head
Perfect Feeling Hits

Is Too Drunk To Drive
Calls His Father For A Ride
Starting To Feel Sick

He Hears Their Lecture
Warns Of Family Addiction
The Words Sink In Deep

Year 18

Still In Love With Her
She Shows Her Love To Him Too
Happy And Content

A Junior In School
Applies To The Best Of Schools
Hopeful And Nervous

Dean's List Every Time
Dual Enrollment Classes
Wanting To Succeed

Watches The War Start
Freeing Kuwait From Iraq
First War In His Time

Visits Florida
Space Shuttle Atlantis Launch
Exciting To See

Level Three Achieved
Making His Own Rockets Soar
Loving Rocketry

Impresses Teachers
Great Analytical Mind
Destined For Greatness

Year 19

Now A Full Adult
Now A Senior In High School
No Longer A Child

Engineering Goal
Accepted By M.I.T
Partial Scholarship

Girl Sad And Happy
Parents Congratulate Him
Soon He Will Be Gone

Distance Starts To Grow
The Tensions Rise Between Them
 Fearing The Future

She Fears The Distance
He Asks Her To Come With Him
She Is Hesitant

He Thinks About It
Cries In Fear Of Losing Her
It Is Up To Her

They Watch Robin Hood
'Everything I Do' Hits Them
She Will Go With Him

Graduates Honors
The Valedictorian
Mom Cries, Dad Is Proud

Year 20

He Starts M.I.T.
She Enrolls, Junior College
They Are Together

A Small Apartment
Paid For By His Mom And Dad
They Both Call It Home

Better Than He Hoped
Has Strong Academic Start
Path Is Clear To Him

His Love Of Her Grows
They Study And Party Too
She Is His Whole World

Cruising Through The Days
His Life On Autopilot
He Lets Down His Guard

The Phone Ring Early
His Mother Is Crying Hard
His Father Is Dead

Betrayed By His Heart
Found On The Dining Room Floor
His Dad Stricken Down

Grief Swells In His Heart
Shocked By The News Of His Death
He Begins To Sob

She Embraces Him
Comfort To His Damaged Soul
He Is Overwhelmed

Mind Races Around
In Disbelief And Sadness
He Cries With His Mom

Stands At The Altar
Still Numb, Angry, And Upset
Gives His Eulogy

He Looks At His Mom
Begins To Cry For Her Loss
Full Of Emotion

Uncertain Of God
How Could He Do This To Him
Angry And Hateful

Something Now Has Changed
His Heart Begins To Harden
Sheltered Life Destroyed

Year 21

He Still Studies Hard
His Passion Has Diminished
Still Struggling With Death

She Is Still Shutout
Trying To Get Past It All
Failing To Do So

Their Life Together
Changed By His Dad's Sudden Death
She Is Hanging In

Life Is Still Shattered
His Mom Is Suffering Worse
Consumed With Sorrow

Stops Going To Church
His Lost Soul Is In Darkness
Resentment Of God

His Love Prays For Him
She Is Worried And Concerned
He Does Not Notice

Months Have Now Passed By
Time Passes, Slowly Healing
Soul Is Still Hardened

She Still Supports Him
Her Love Is Giving Him Hope
He Is Coming Back

Mind Is Clearing Up
Studies Return To Normal
Sadness In Control

He Gets On One Knee
Knows She Is The One For Him
She Accepts With Tears

Year 22

Now In His Third Year
Living Their Life Together
Wedding Approaches

Life Almost Normal
Mother Has Grown So Distant
Words Are Slurred Most Days

Talks To Mom Daily
She Is Still Not Coping Well
Her Soulmate Is Dead

Worries About Her
Many Ways, So Far Away
Asks Her To Get Help

Reenters The Church
No Longer Angry With Him
Thanks God For His Life

Life Is Back On Course
Living His Life On Life's Terms
Struggle Mostly Won

Year 23

Now In His Fourth Year
Going To Get A Masters
Wedding Coming Up

Mom Will Not Be There
She Says She Is Too Busy
She Is Still Too Sad

Lost In Her Sorrow
Mom Unable To Move On
He Tried To Help Her

He Fails To Do So
She Refuses Help From Him
Loves Only Self Hate

Nervous And Joyful
Self-Written Vows Of True Love
They Both Cry With Joy

Their Love Is Bonded
Celebrated With Loved Ones
Most Of Them Are There

They Buy A New House
Enough Room For The Baby
She Is Now With Child

Her Parents Happy
They Have Created A Life
Mom Seems Not To Care

He Gets Internship
Large Chip Manufacturer
She Stays Home For Now

He Continues School
She Enjoys The Pregnancy
Happiness Feeds Them

Two Souls Turned To One
Now The One Makes A Second
Their Love Binds Their Soul

Life Progresses On
Expanding Their Souls And Love
God's Blessing On Them

Year 24

Baby Soon To Come
Much Excitement In The Air
Nursery Ready

A Tragedy Strikes
Oklahoma Explosion
Many Children Killed

Her Labor Begins
A Beautiful Baby Boy
Named After His Dad

He Calls His Mother
She Begins To Cry, Hangs Up
He Is Not Surprised

Her Parents Are Thrilled
His Aunt Calls, Mom Slit Her Wrists
She Bled Out Alone

He Is Taken Back
Joy Has Now Turned To Sorrow
His Mother Is Dead

A Birth And A Death
Two Life Events On One Day
Birth Wins Over Death

Happy About Birth
He Is Saddened By Her Death
Her Pain Is Now Gone

They Embrace Their Love
They Thank God For Each Other
They Love Their Baby

He Buries Mother
He Stands Alone At Their Graves
Both Parents Now Gone

May God Have Mercy
He Hopes Her Pain Is Over
Her Suicide Sin

Year 25

Continuing School
Moving Up In His Career
Still Dreams Of Rockets

She Is Back To Work
Able To Set Her Own Hours
Home With The Baby

Probate Is Over
Inheritance Pays Off House
Student Loans And Car

Finances Are Set
Wants To Intern With NASA
Soon A Dream Fulfilled

Her Parents Are Close
They Take Him In As Their Own
Has Parents Again

Last Few Years Were Tough
Feels The Love He Has Needed
Parental Figures

Part Of His Soul Heals
Her Family Now Is His
Loving And Gracious

Internship Approved
His Dream Of NASA Is Here
Family Is Proud

Year 26

Not A Lot Of Time
He Works Hard And Goes To School
She Understands It

He Has His Dream Job
Sending People Into Space
For Exploration

The Baby Gets Big
He Wishes He Was Home More
His Work Betters Man

She Grows Her Business
Her Own Person, But Still One
They Work As A Team

Support Each Other
Together Through Thick And Thin
Each Other's Best Friend

She Makes Him Dinner
Always Loving Each Other
He Gives Her Flowers

He Thinks About Them
Smiles About Their Love They Had
Parents Once Happy

It Ended So Sad
She Could Not Move On From Love
Her Heart Died With Them

He Visits Their Grave
Tells Them All About His Life
He Hopes They Can Hear

A New Perspective
He Watches The Shuttle Launch
Seems So Different

He Looks Back At Life
So Many Good Times For Him
His Life Has Been Good

Year 27

School Is Almost Done
NASA, Better Than His Dream
His Wife Fills His Heart

Her Brother Visits
Announces That He Is Gay
Her Parents Are Shocked

They Take It In Stride
He Had Told Her Years Ago
She Held His Secret

She Loves Family
He Looks Proudly At His Wife
Loves Her Loyalty

He Sees It Clearly
This Is What Family Is
Unconditional

He Wonders At Man
Sheppard Killed For Being Gay
Two Embassies Bombed

He Fears For His Child
He Sees The Hate In The World
Wants More For His Son

He And His Wife Pray
For Love, Peace, And Happiness
Their Love Of God Grows

Year 28

He Finishes School
New Millennium Coming
Turn Of Century

He Is Promoted
Working On Shuttle Program
Dream Almost Complete

On The Mission Floor
He Helps Discovery Dock
First Time With Station

She Is Proud Of Him
He Is Excited For Weeks
Life So Fulfilling

Mars Lander Crashes
Engines Prematurely Stop
Work Getting Stressful

They Thank God Often
They Feel His Grace Upon Them
Blessed Lives They Do Live

The New Year Rolls In
They Celebrate With Their Friends
The World Does Not End

Year 29

He Plays With His Child
They Tell Him About Jesus
Teaches Him God's Love

She Helps Their Pastor
They Grow Active In Their Church
Helping Spread The Word

Hundredth Shuttle Flight
He Is Brought To Tears At Launch
He Is So Thankful

His Son Starts Baseball
He Struggles But Loves The Game
He Does Well Enough

Her Parents Visit
He Now Calls Them Mom And Dad
He Is Like Their Son

They Ask About Work
They Share In Their Happiness
Their Lives Being Shared

He Watches His Son
He Sees His In-Laws With Him
There is Some Pain Felt

Year 30

After Fifteen Years
The MIR Space Station Returns
Plummets Back To Earth

He Watches At Work
Not American, Still Sad
End Of An Era

He Takes Vacation
They All Go To Disney World
His Son Is In Awe

He Drinks His Coffee
News Report Interrupts Him
Plane Strikes North Tower

He Is Shocked By It
A Terrible Accident
South Tower Is Struck

His Eyes Fill With Tears
Realizes What This Is
An Attack On Us

The Breakroom Fills Up
The Pentagon Struck As Well
People Are Upset

Fear Builds In The Room
Is NASA A Target Too
Some People Leave Work

He Decides To Stay
He Monitors Space Assets
He Watches Updates

South Tower Comes Down
The Image Makes His Legs Weak
North Tower Comes Down

His Wife Calls Upset
They Can't Contact Her Brother
He Is In New York

He And His Wife Watch
They Watch The President Speak
Their Hearts Are Heavy

They Embrace God's Love
They Find Comfort In His Grace
World Forever Changed

Her Brother Feared Dead
She Is Overwhelmed With Grief
His Turn To Help Her

Days Pass With No News
Each Day There Is Less Hope Left
Brother Presumed Dead

She Is Tormented
Not Knowing For Sure His Fate
No Body To Mourn

She Prays For Comfort
God Answers Through Her Husband
He Knows What To Say

He Knows How She Feels
He Has Suffered His Own Loss
He Is There For Her

Family Gathers
Bury An Empty Casket
Body Never Found

Year 31

He Begins To Coach
Wants To Teach Them Sportsmanship
His Son's Baseball Team

She Is On The Mend
His Wife Is Feeling Better
Still Sad But Better

Her Parents Struggle
They Are Sad And Still Angry
They Are Still Healing

A Pain Hard To Grasp
Nothing Like Losing A Child
Grief Like No Other

He Enjoys NASA
He Is Promoted Again
Advancing Up Fast

He And His Wife Try
Want To Have Another Child
They Hope For A Girl

Year 32

He Is At The Launch
Columbia Leaves The Pad
Foam Strikes The Shuttle

He Reviews Data
Foam Strikes Are Not Uncommon
Team Asks For Photos

Photo Request Stopped
Shuttle Had Been Struck Before
Deemed Low-Risk Event

He Was Not Worried
He Watched The Flight Return Home
News Reports Started

Upon Reentry
The Shuttle Disintegrates
All Of The Crew Lost

He Feels Guilt And Loss
Should Have Done It Different
He Has Failed The Crew

His Wife Consoles Him
He Feels The Weight Of Their Death
He Is Now Distant

She Tries To Reach Him
He Is Angry And Upset
Cannot Eat Or Sleep

The Guilt Starts To Fade
Mistakes Were Made, Not By Him
Above His Pay Grade

Fighting Their Own Pain
They Fail To Conceive A Child
Their Faith Carries Them

Year 33

He Works Late Often
Rebuilding Shuttle Program
Doing What He Can

New Safety Measures
He Helps Ensure Crew Safety
Hard But Rewarding

He Takes His Son Out
They Have Fifty Yard Line Seats
His First Football Game

Denver Beats Tampa
They Eat Hot Dogs And Popcorn
They Laugh And Have Fun

His Wife Looks Ashen
She Has Not Felt Well Lately
She Gets A Checkup

She Has Become Sick
Diagnosed, Leukemia
She Is Terrified

They Cry Together
The Doctor Offers Some Hope
Treatment Starts Quickly

He Fears She Will Die
She Has Faith She Will Survive
His Faith Is Tested

Year 34

Round Four Of Chemo
Her Final Round Of Treatment
They Are Both Hopeful

She Has Lost Her Hair
Their Son Does Not Understand
Often Has Nightmares

Prayer Circle Prays
Regardless Of The Outcome
They Ask God For Strength

She Does Not Fear Death
She Fears The Pain Of Dying
She Fears For Her Son

Distracted From Work
He Takes A Leave Of Absence
They Are Supportive

He Does Not Notice
He Misses Deep Impact Launch
Wife Only Focus

She Wears A Blue Scarf
She Struggles Being So Weak
She Is Now Rail Thin

He Comforts His Wife
Space Shuttle Returns To Flight
Watches On The News

He Keeps Wondering
A Life Without Her In It
His Faith Is Not Strong

Her Chemo Is Done
She Goes Into Remission
Burden Is Lifted

Her Parents Relieved
They Are All Grateful To God
They Have Persevered

Year 35

He Plays With His Son
They Go To A Baseball Game
The Devil Rays Lose

He Is Getting Big
They Talk On The Way Back Home
Building Memories

He Is Back To Work
He Appreciates It More
A New Lease On Life

She Is Gaining Strength
He Still Fears It Will Return
Her Hair Is Growing

It Has Been Five Years
His Wife Visits Ground Zero
Her Parents With Her

They Mourn Her Brother
She Cries And Screams At The Site
She Lets Out Her Pain

Her Soul Has Lifted
She Finally Has Closure
Her Burden Released

Year 36

They Go To Aspen
They Ski And Make A Snowman
Just The Three Of Them

A Warm Summer Day
They Watch Their Son Play Baseball
He Is Improving

She Becomes Pregnant
The Two Of Them Are Surprised
Thought Time Had Passed Them

She Calls Her Parents
They Are Happy For Them Both
They Thank God, Praise Him

Their Son Is Happy
Wants To Be A Good Brother
Excitement By All

New Life Brings New Hope
Children Are Blessings From God
God's Eternal Love

Year 37

They Are All Upset
Father And Son At Her Bed
Still Recovering

The Baby Is Lost
They All Feel The Pain Deeply
Only Twelve Weeks Left

Her Faith Remains Strong
His Faith Shaken But Not Gone
God Always Has Plans

He Continues On
He Talks With His Old Pastor
He Is Comforted

Life Starts To Resume
They Carry On Together
They Are Still In Love

Facing Life's Troubles
Their Bond Is Unbreakable
Two People, One Soul

Year 38

He Is On A Break
He Watches A Miracle
Placed Down By God's Hand

All Passengers Safe
Jet Lands In Hudson River
Pilot A Hero

His Wife Starts Teaching
At Community College
She Wants To Give Back

Her Cousin Moves In
She Is Rebuilding Her Life
Fresh Out Of Rehab

She Has Battled Long
She Has Found God In The Rooms
She Looks Good And Strong

He And His Wife Hope
Offer Her Support And Love
A Troubled Soul Found

Year 39

Her Cousin Is Well
They Are Very Proud Of Her
She Has Embraced God

Avatar Calls Them
They Have Seen It Four Times Now
Family Outings

She Works Through The Steps
She Has Just Gotten A Job
She Helps At The House

He Sees So Much Loss
Human And Sea Life Destroyed
Oil Rig Explosion

He Watches From Work
He Watches Falcon Nine Launch
Maiden Flight Success

Supportive Of Flight
Exciting Fresh Ideas
New Innovations

He Is Excited
New Project Rumors At Work
Has Some Ideas

Year 40

He Is Selected
NASA's Space Launch System Team
New Space Vehicle

He Tells Wife And Son
His Wife Is Happy For Him
High Five From His Son

Atlantis Shuttle
Orbiters Discontinued
The Program's Last Flight

Their Son Makes A Choice
Confirmation Class Begins
Showing God His Love

They Are Glad For Him
No Pressure It Was His Choice
Parents And God's Love

Her Cousin Works Hard
She Is Leading A Meeting
Renewed Sober Life

Year 41

Dragon Crew Launches
First Commercial Crew Docking
He Is Astonished

He Works Long Hours Now
Focusing On S.L.S
Passioned By The Work

Her Cousin Moves Out
Recovery Progressing
She Often Visits

Their Son Is Confirmed
Later Than Most, But His Time
Proud Of Their Son's Choice

She Is Empowered
Fulfilled By Teaching Others
Has Found Her Calling

His Soul Weeps And Hurts
Children Killed At Sandy Hook
Satan's Handy Work

Year 42

Not A Catholic
Impressed By Pope Selection
He Likes The New Pope

Bombing In Boston
She Remembers Her Brother
Feels For Families

He Hugs Her, She Cries
Sometimes It Still Hits Her Hard
He Feels For Her Pain

He Is Frustrated
Progress At Work Slow Going
Already Behind

Their Son Is Eighteen
He Enlists In The Army
Wants To Serve Country

Feels This Is His Path
His Dad Is Proud Of His Choice
Mom Worries For Him

Year 43

She Takes On More Work
He Is Making Some Progress
Both Enjoy Their Work

Their Son Is Murdered
Killed At The Fort Hood Shooting
He Died Instantly

Funeral Was Hard
They Cried Like Never Before
Pastor Gave Comfort

His Life Gone Too Soon
All Of The Things He Will Miss
The Things They Will Miss

The Two Carry On
Rely On Their Faith And Love
They Hold Each Other

All Part Of God's Plan
They Do Not Understand It
They Do Accept It

Both Continue On
They Wait For The Pain To Ease
As They Know It Will

Year 44

They Stumble Forward
Their Heart Still Open And Raw
Still Coming To Terms

The Pain Seems Endless
They Keep Praying For The Strength
Each Day Seems Empty

Numb And Still Hurting
Going Through Motions Of Life
They Work, And They Sleep

Slowly A Peace Comes
Things Start To Feel Livable
Hurt Will Never Leave

Water Found On Mars
He Sees Possibilities
Water Means Fuel

Falcon Booster Lands
He Never Thought Possible
Remarkable Feat

He Travels Back Home
He Visits His Parents Graves
He Pours Out His Soul

He Hopes They Hear Him
He Feels A Sense Of Release
He Feels Much Better

Year 45

The House Feels Empty
It Is Just The Two Of Them
They Grow Closer Still

Celebrate Their Love
Before Friends And Family
They Renew Their Vows

They Go To New York
Fifteen Years Have Now Gone By
She Remembers Him

They Look Back On Life
All Of The Love And Heart Aches
Both Tested And Blessed

NASA Is Old School
He Tries To Cut The Red Tape
Set In Their Old Ways

He Thinks Of Leaving
To Join The Falcon Nine Team
He Decides To Stay

Year 46

He Is Reassigned
Different Part Of NASA
Project Artemis

A Bold New Project
Mankind's Return To The Moon
Passion Is Renewed

His Wife Supports Him
She Sees His Love For His Work
She Is Always There

They Host A Party
The Night Is Filled With Laughter
Their Stress Is Relieved

Her Cousin Is Well
She Is Getting Married Soon
Her Life Rebuilding

He Is A Writer
A Freelance News Reporter
They Seem Well Suited

Year 47

Falcon Heavy Launch
Powerful And Amazing
He Watches It Soar

Her Parents Visit
They Talk And Laugh Together
A Good Distraction

They Enjoy Their Time
Her Parents Stay For A Week
Good To Have Around

She Volunteers Now
Helping People Deal With Grief
Finds It Rewarding

He Fights With NASA
Trying To Move Things Along
So Many Delays

Progress Is Slowing
Always Such A Slow Pace Set
Government At Work

Year 48

She Asks Him To Help
He Decides To Volunteer
Together They Help

Both Enjoy Helping
They Find It Therapeutic
Giving Something Back

Sharing In God's Love
Working To Relieve Their Pain
Sharing About Loss

He Works For Space Force
New Military Branch Formed
Name Makes Him Chuckle

They Watch The Sunset
Lowering To The Water
See God In The Light

Like Seeing Heaven
Calm, Warm, A Heavenly Light
Relaxing The Soul

Year 49

Disease Starts To Spread
Cases Are Growing Daily
Concern Is Starting

The School Closes Down
She Stays At Home And Inside
People Are Dying

He Works Remotely
He Is Concerned For Her Health
He Could Not Lose Her

The Pandemic Grows
He Shops For What He Can Get
He Takes Precautions

Her Father Is Sick
Her Mother Cannot See Him
She Worries For Them

He Worries For Her
Call They Feared Finally Comes
Her Father Has Passed

She Talks To Her Mom
They Suffer Another Loss
Together They Cry

He Comforts Them Both
Her Mother Worries For Them
They Worry For Her

He Is Pleased With Work
NASA And SpaceX Talk Mars
Space Future Hopeful

Trump Pushes Vaccine
Vaccines Come In Record Time
They See Things Improve

Year 50

A New President
Worries About Budget Cuts
Has Happened Before

She Teaches From Home
He Returns To The Office
Things Are Not As Bad

People Still Wear Masks
He Is A Firm Believer
Always Wears One Out

She Visits Her Mom
They Hold A Memorial
She Says Her Goodbyes

She Misses Her Dad
Her Mother Is Doing Well
A Surreal Year

After Two Decades
He Watches The James Webb Launch
New Space Telescope

Year 51

Watches It Rollout
Testing For S.L.S. Starts
Watching, He Is Proud

Testing Has Failures
He Sees It As A Setback
They Work The Problem

He Suggests They Move
A Smaller House, Less Upkeep
She Agrees With Him

His House Sells Quickly
They Get A Place On The Beach
Two Bedroom Condo

He Is Close To Work
They Love Living On The Beach
She Loves Laying Out

They Still Mourn Their Son
Wondering What Could Have Been
They Miss Him So Much

Short Life Filled With Love
They Talk About Him Often
Remembering Him

Year 52

His Day Has Arrived
S.L.S. Has Flawless Launch
He Feels Accomplished

She Goes On Church Trip
She Travels To Israel
Sees The Holy Land

Every Day He Swims
He Loves The Salty Ocean
Loves The Exercise

He Lost Twenty Pounds
Best Shape He Has Been In Years
Enjoying His Life

Housewarming Party
Showing Off Their New Beach House
All Of Their Friends Come

They Sponsor A Trip
Church Is Going To Haiti
Going To Build Schools

Keeping The Feeling
Giving The Glory To God
Finding Love And Peace

Year 53

She Is Tutoring
Her Cousin Comes To Visit
Still Married And Clean

Still Goes To Meetings
Her Cousin Is Doing Well
Thanks Them For Their Help

He Watches The Launch
First Crewed Starship Orbits Earth
Largest Manned Rocket

He Buys A Tesla
His First All Electric Car
He Loves How It Drives

They Swim Together
Keeping Healthy And Happy
Eating The Right Food

They Watch The Sun Set
Often While Eating Dinner
Feeling Ocean Breeze

Year 54

On To The Next Faze
S.L.S. Artemis Two
NASA Moon Test Flight

He Is Second Lead
He Continues To Work Hard
Rising Up The Ranks

Church Keeps Her Busy
On Selection Committee
Finding A New Priest

They Are Still Active
They Enjoy Going To Church
They Still Feel God's Love

Never Questioning
Their Faith Stronger Than Ever
Bound In Faith By Love

They Place Flowers Down
They Cry At Their Son's Grave Site
They Miss Him Always

Year 55

She Sees The Doctor
She Has Not Been Feeling Well
The News Is Not Good

She Already Knew
She Had Been Feeling Rundown
Her Cancer Is Back

Prognosis Not Good
The Cancer Is More Advanced
She Starts On Chemo

He Is By Her Side
She Is Not Responding Well
They Pray And Fight It

She Is Still Hopeful
He Is Scared He Might Lose Her
They Pray, And They Cry

She Grows Weaker Fast
The Doctors Are Not Hopeful
They Say Six Months More

She Takes It In Stride
He Fears Losing His True Love
She Is Making Peace

He Tells Her To Fight
He Puts All His Work On Hold
She Stays Strong For Him

Work Has Him On Leave
She Is His Only Focus
Nothing Else Matters

She Still Gets Treatment
They Spend Their Time On The Beach
Exchanging Their Love

She Has Peace Of Mind
He Sees Her Slipping Away
His Heart Is Breaking

Year 56

She Is Hanging On
Some Days Are Good; Some Are Not
It Is Up And Down

He Dares To Have Hope
He Tries To Be Strong For Her
He Prays For Healing

He Cannot Lose Her
She Tells Him It Is Okay
He Lives In His Fear

Friends Come To Visit
She Is Stronger Than He Is
People Pray With Them

The Church Is Helpful
They Make Sure Their Needs Are Met
Prayers, Love, And Hope

Six Months Come And Gone
She Continues To Hold On
The Pain Is Constant

She Struggles Each Day
Growing Weaker And Thinner
She Is Thin And Gaunt

They Pray For Relief
They Know The End Is Nearing
They Pray For Mercy

They Watch The Sun Set
He Is Kneeling Next To Her
Breathing Gets Shallow

He Sees Her Eyes Close
He Is Holding Her Frail Hand
Her Breathing Fades Out

She Has Returned Home
She Has Entered The Kingdom
She Is Now At Peace

His Tears Are Streaming
He Gently Rubs Her Still Face
He Still Holds Her Hand

He Gets Off His Knees
A Soft Kiss To Her Forehead
He Tells Her Goodbye

Year 57

He Sits On The Couch
He Still Has His Black Suit On
All Alone He Cries

A Large Gathering
Funeral Was Beautiful
He Misses Her So

He Stays On His Leave
He Contemplates What To Do
Unsure Of Next Move

He Talks With Pastor
Finds A Worthy Distraction
Missionary Work

Going To Build Schools
Dominican Republic
A Sabbatical

He Loves The Work There
Finally Starting To Feel
He Can Smile Again

Year 58

He Finds His Calling
Now Is The Time To Retire
New Path For New Life

He Works In The Sun
Building Houses, Not Rockets
He Learns Building Skills

Work Is Rewarding
Helping Those Who Need It Most
He Loves The People

Feels God Around Him
He Attends A Little Church
God Working Through Him

Working With Locals
Living In A Little Town
Enjoying New Hope

He Still Misses Her
She Is Always In His Heart
Pain Has Receded

Pleased With His New Path
He Embraces These People
Serenity Found

Still Coping With Loss
He Wishes She Was With Him
A Piece Of Him Gone

Year 59

So Much Poverty
Houses Nothing More Than Shacks
Vacationers Blind

He Is So Humbled
Changed By The Experience
He Tutors Children

He Talks With Adults
He Plays Games With The Children
He Lives With Them All

New Levels Of Peace
Through The Miracle Of God
Found Within Their Hearts

Returns To Visit
Travels Back To Florida
Sees Old NASA Friends

He Is Received Well
They Comment On His Freedom
Seeing He Has Changed

He Enjoyed The Trip
Returns Back To The D.R.
Back Where He Belongs

Year 60

He Prays And Helps Build
A Labor Of Love And Hope
Opens Medical Clinic

He Works With Doctors
Volunteering A Weeks' Time
A New Foundation

He Does What He Can
Trying To Improve Their Lives
Paying It Forward

Honoring Her Life
Leaving Their Mark On The World
Remembering Her

Most Days, He Is Good
He Can Still Struggle At Times
His Lost Love Still Hurts

He Carries Onward
Not Regretting His Life's Path
Living For Today

Year 61

He Catches The Flu
Needs Hospitalization
Out Three Days Later

Was Pushing Too Hard
Reminds Him He Is Mortal
Going To Scale Back

He Is Still Working
Shorter Hours And Fewer Days
Loves Helping Others

A Much Simpler Life
More Rewarding Than NASA
His True Life's Calling

He Does Not Fear Death
He Wonders When Death Will Come
When Will He See Her

He Thinks Of His Son
Ponders What Life Could Have Been
A Life Cut Too Short

He Thanks God Daily
For The Blessings Of His Life
For Sending His Grace

Year 62

He Hits The Ground Hard
Twenty-Foot Drop From Above
Lost Footing On Roof

His Leg Screams In Pain
Searing Hot Pain On Right Side
He Cannot See Straight

Darkness Encroaches
Confusion Taking Over
Sides Narrowing In

Awakes In A Bed
He Hears Beeping Monitors
D.R. Hospital

Doctor Checks On Him
Compound Fracture Of The Leg
Bleeding has been Stopped

Thirty-Four Stitches
Four Pins, Two Plates, And High Pain
He Will Recover

Feels The Pain Of It
He Embraces Therapy
It Will Take Some Time

Year 63

Returns To The Site
The Clinic Almost Complete
It Has Been Two Months

People Come To Him
Happy He Is Back And Well
He Uses A Cane

He Gets Around Well
The Pain Is Manageable
Peaceful And Content

They Ask About Him
He Tells Them About His Care
That He Had Missed Them

They Have Block Party
Salpicon And Goat Chenchen
His Two Favorites

He Feels Real Love
Part Of Their Community
Wishes She Was Here

Year 64

He Is Without Her
He Carries Her In His Heart
Always On His Mind

New To Some Of Them
Shows Them How To Play Baseball
He Coaches The Kids

The Kids Enjoy It
Reminds Him Of Time With Son
Time With His Father

Finding Memories
The Memories Of His Past
Fondness Of Days Past

The Women Teach Him
He Learns To Cook Local Food
Reminds Him Of Mom

He Remembers Them
Memories Keep Them Alive
Will Never Forget

He Loves The Culture
Rich With Family Values
Different Than His

He Sees Days Later
The Mission To Mars Has Launched
He Smiles To Himself

Year 65

He Leaves The D.R.
Is Time For Him To Move On
He Will Visit Them

He Buys A Cabin
In Jackson Hole Wyoming
Beautiful Landscape

He Enjoys The Air
Cool, Crisp, Clean, And Refreshing
Something New To Him

He Has Good Neighbors
Lots Of Things For Him To Do
They Show Him Around

He Likes To Hike Trails
Exploring Grand Teton Park
Wilderness Untouched

His Cabin Is Small
Some Would Say It Is Cozy
He Calls It Perfect

Temperatures Drop
He Enjoys The Cold Winter
He Warms By The Fire

Year 66

He Does Not Feel Well
His Chest Feels Tight And Heavy
His Left Arm Is Sore

Doctors Check Him Out
He Has Had A Heart Attack
It Is A Mild One

They Place In Three Stents
No Permanent Damage Done
He Recovers Well

He Returns Back Home
Decides To Take It Easy
He Does Not Worry

He Likes His New Church
Different Than His Others
More Fundamental

Invigorates Him
He Sees The Fun Side Of God
Celebrating God

Year 67

The Winter Sets In
He Decides To Start Writing
Non-Fiction Novel

He Writes About Life
He Writes For Himself Alone
His Journey Through Life

His Path Written Down
His Life's Struggles And Blessings
His Accomplishments

His Failures In Life
The Loss Of His Wife And Son
His Belief In God

The Process Calms Him
Writing Helps Him Remember
Gives Him Inner Peace

He Shares Some Of It
Lets His Neighbor Read Highlights
They Seem To Like It

Year 68

He Found A Passion
Writing Has Been Rewarding
He Continues On

He Writes For Himself
It Is For The Ones He Lost
Honoring Their Life

The Book Releases
Sales Are Low, Reviews Are Great
He Is Fine With That

He Receives Emails
People Asking Him Questions
How It Affects Them

People Finding Hope
He Finds It Touches People
The Book Is Profound

He Takes A Road Trip
Travels Around The Country
He Takes In The Sights

Year 69

Starts California
He Sees San Francisco Bay
Heads South To L.A.

Next Arizona
He Visits The Grand Canyon
Stops In Sedona

Spends Time In Utah
National Parks In Moab
Peaceful And Serene

Colorado Bound
He Visits The Grand Mesa
He Enjoys Moose Day

In New Mexico
He Views The Carlsbad Caverns
He Enjoys It All

Cowboy Museum
Oklahoma Delights Him
Philbrook Museum

He Is In No Rush
Kansas Wichita Gardens
Keeper Of The Plains

The Sunken Gardens
Union Pacific Railroad
He Takes It All In

Visits Mount Rushmore
He Sees Whatever He Wants
He Continues On

The Dakota Zoo
Roosevelt National Park
Documents It All

Goes To The Big Sky
Museum Of The Rockies
Sees Lamar Valley

Chihuly Gardens
Museum Of Flight Lifts Him
Sees Mount St. Helens

Columbia Gorge

Portland Japanese Garden

He Travels Back Home

Year 70

He Enjoyed His Trip
He Wishes She Had Been There
He Is Home Alone

He Cleans Up The Place
It Has That Empty Stale Smell
It Airs Out Nicely

He Meets With His Friends
He Tells Them Of His Travels
He Shares His Pictures

His Time Seems Endless
Tries To Fill The Empty Hours
He Tutors In Math

He Enjoys Teaching
Helping Those Learn What He Knows
Teaching Like His Wife

He Likes The Feeling
The Passing Of His Knowledge
Gives Him A Purpose

Year 71

He Feels The Years Now
He Gets Tired Much Easier
He Is Getting Old

His Joints Hurt Badly
Damaged And Worn Through The Years
Feeling His Old Age

The Cold Makes It Worse
He Rents A Small Apartment
Back In Florida

The Warmer Air Helps
Still Sore, But There Is Relief
He Talks To Old Friends

They Catch Up On Things
Hears About Their Families
They Talk About Mars

It Is Nice To Hear
Missed Talking With Old Work Friends
He Misses NASA

He Walks Down The Beach
Stares Out Over The Ocean
He Missed The Ocean

Year 72

He Sees His Doctor
Has Arthritis In His Joints
Warm Air Is Helping

His Heart Checks Out Fine
Doctor Gives Clean Bill Of Health
Blood Tests Are Normal

He Goes To A Game
Sees The Rays Beat The Yankees
Thinks About His Son

Drives By The Old House
He Looks At It With Fondness
Good Memories Here

Plays Chess In The Park
He Enjoys Playing Again
Worthy Opponent

He Wanders Around
Looking For Things To Fill Time
He Is Passing Time

Year 73

He Still Goes To Church
Usually Twice A Week
He Finds Comfort There

He Stops By Often
Has Coffee With The Pastor
They Talk About Life

He Watches The News
Politicians Still Lying
People Still Killing

The World Advances
He Knows That People Do Not
It Is Getting Worse

He Sees Lost People
The Decline In Religion
They Go Hand In Hand

Things Always Changing
Just Never For The Better
He Sighs In Disgust

Year 74

He Goes To Georgia
He Visits His Wife's Cousin
Enjoys Seeing Her

She Is Doing Good
They Talk About The Old Times
They Trade Old Stories

She Is Still Sober
His Wife Would Be Proud Of Her
She Has A Good Life

He Stays For Three Days
It Makes Him Feel More At Ease
He Hugs Her Goodbye

Time Passes Slowly

Too Many Hours In The Day

His Days Just Drag On

Sometimes He Will Write

He Reads Books Most Of The Day

He Keeps A Journal

Year 75

He Goes Wine Tasting
Friends From NASA Take Him Out
He Never Drank Much

He Enjoys The Day
Not The Wine But Time With Friends
They Go Out To Eat

He Has Fun Again
He Knows He Needs To Get Out
Spend More Time With Friends

He Has Been Thinking
He Joins A Rocketry Club
He Helps People Build

He Is Popular
Real Rocket Scientist
People Pick His Brain

Some Things Never Change
He Likes Seeing Rockets Launch
Back To His Passion

Year 76

He Is Sleeping More
He Continues To Slow Down
He Feels Elderly

He Sees His Doctor
The Doctor Says He Is Fine
Confirms It Is Age

He Keeps Going On
Church, Rocketry, And Reading
He Is Satisfied

He Decides To Write
He Writes A Rocketry Guide
Posts It Free Online

He Makes Barbeque
He Goes To A Church Picnic
They Eat And Have Fun

Lots Of People Come
Pastor Gives A Brief Sermon
He Enjoys His Church

Year 77

He Wakes Up Sweaty
He Feels A Pain In His Chest
He Remembers This

He Grabs For His Phone
He Calls 9-1-1 To Help
He Thinks Of His Dad

He Hears The Sirens
He Hears Them Getting Louder
He Is Not Fearful

He Is Not Worried
He Feels At Peace With It All
He Trusts In God's Will

Doctors Work On Him
He Feels It Slipping Away
He Is Losing Ground

He Feels God With Him
He Thinks About What Is Next
Ready To Go Home

His Eyes Slowly Close
The Monitors Are Beeping
The Doctors Scramble

He Feels God Enter
He Can Feel He Is Leaving
His Shell Below Him

Overwhelming Love
Embraces God's Open Arms
Returning To Him

Sees His Wife And Son
They Have Been Waiting For Him
Now Reunited

The Journey Over
A New Journey Now Starting
For Eternity

His Life Had Been Good
What Is Next Will Be Better
Everlasting Love

ABOUT THE AUTHOR

Born in 1973, Brett C Persson is an aspiring poet and recovering alcoholic who crafts his experiences into thought-provoking poetry and prose. As the author of his debut book, "Poetry Of An Addict" and several other collections, Brett hopes to provide readers with poignant insights into the life of a recovering addict as he ranges across universal themes through descriptive wordplay and vivid imagery. He aims to reassure readers who are struggling with alcoholism that they're not alone, helping them find solace in the unique and expressive power of poetry. Brett currently resides in Buckeye, Arizona with his wonderful wife and three daughters.

11/14/2011